Garfield's PET FORCE™

PIE-RAT'S REVENGE!

Garfield's PET FORCE™
PIE-RAT'S REVENGE!

Created by
Jim Davis

Character development by
Mark Acey & Gary Barker

Written by
Michael Teitelbaum

Illustrated by
Gary Barker & Larry Fentz

SCHOLASTIC INC.
New York Toronto London Auckland Sydney

Produced by Creative Media Applications, Inc. and Paws Inc.
Additional Inking by Lori Barker
Graphics by Jeff Wesley

ISBN 0-590-05909-2

12 11 10 9 8 7   0 1 2/0

Printed in the U.S.A.   40

First Scholastic printing, November 1997

Introduction

When a group of lovable pets — Garfield, Odie, Arlene, Nermal, and Pooky — are transported to an alternate universe, they become a mighty superhero team known as . . . *Pet Force!*

Garzooka — Large and in charge, he is the fearless and famished leader of Pet Force. He's a ferocious feline with nerves of steel, a razor-sharp right claw, and the awesome ability to fire gamma-radiated hairballs (as well as deadly one-liners) from his mouth.

Odious — Although utterly clueless, he possesses incredible strength, ultra-slippery slobber, and a super-stretchy stun tongue. One zap of his lethal wet tongue causes a total mental meltdown in anyone he unleashes it upon.

Starlena — Sings a *purrfectly* pitched siren song ("the meow that wows!"). Anyone who hears her hypnotic song immediately falls into a trance — except Garzooka.

Abnermal — Has a body temperature of absolute zero; one touch of his icy paw freezes foes in their tracks. He can extend a nuke-proof force field to protect himself, as well as the other Pet Force members. His pester-power — more annoying than your little brother! — is one power that Garzooka could live without.

Compooky — Part-computer, part-teddy, this cyberbear extraordinaire is not only incredibly cute, but is also the mental giant of the team (not that big a deal).

Behold the mighty Pet Force! *Let the fur fly!*

Garfield's
PET FORCE™

Pie-Rat's
REVENGE!

1

The story so far . . .

There exist an infinite number of universes parallel to our own. Each one is similar to ours, but each one is also unique in its own way. In one such parallel universe, a group of superheroes known as Pet Force kept the peace for many years. Each of the five members of Pet Force possessed incredible superpowers that they used to battle evil.

Recently, however, an evil veterinarian with magical powers named Vetvix defeated Pet Force, banishing the five heroes to a ghostly dimension from which there is no escape. The kind and benevolent ruler of this alternate universe, Emperor Jon, lived on a peaceful planet known as Polyester. He called upon his sorcerer — Sorcerer Binky — to find new beings to serve as Pet Force.

Using his magic cauldron, Sorcerer Binky opened a doorway between Emperor Jon's universe and our universe. He brought Garfield, Odie, Arlene, Nermal, and Pooky into the parallel universe where *they* took on the powers and appearance of Pet Force. This newly reformed Pet Force defeated Vetvix and her food-loving henchman Space Pie-Rat, but not before Vetvix used her dark magic to change Space Pie-Rat into a tiny white mouse, and then make her escape. Space Pie-Rat, as a mouse, was brought to Emperor Jon and placed in a small cage in his palace.

Garfield and his friends were transported back through the dimensional doorway and returned to their home on Earth in our universe. And for a little while all was right in Emperor Jon's universe.

But only for a little while!

2

The parallel universe . . .

The chiming clock on the wall of Emperor Jon's throne room in his palace on the planet Polyester rang out seven times. The little white mouse, whose tiny body contained the mind of Space Pie-Rat, paced back and forth in his cramped cage.

Pie-Rat heard the door to the throne room open. He cringed as he did each day when Emperor Jon came bounding into the room singing and talking to Pie-Rat in his baby voice.

"The mousy gets his food, the mousy gets his food. Hi-ho the stereo, the mousy gets his food!" sang Emperor Jon.

It's "derio," thought Pie-Rat, whose mind had not been altered despite his tiny mouse body. *Hi-ho the "derio," not "stereo," you idiot! Every day he gets it wrong! I can't stand it!*

"Hello, little mousy," cried out Emperor Jon in a

high-pitched, singsong voice. "It's seven o'clock. Is mousy-wousy weady for his wittle tiny dinner?" he added in the type of baby talk that probably makes even babies want to be sick.

Oh, he's going to make me barf with that stupid baby talk, thought Pie-Rat. *He waltzes in here all happy and singing, and I'm supposed to jump for joy at the prospect of another delicious dinner of cardboard pencil erasers!*

Emperor Jon had grown quite fond of the tiny mouse. He had come to think of the creature as a gentle little pet, almost completely forgetting that this cute and harmless mouse had once been a six-foot-tall, vicious villain who had terrorized his universe. It was Jon's affection for the creature that Pie-Rat was counting on to help make his escape.

If things go my way, this will be the last night I have to force down those disgusting doodads he calls food! thought Pie-Rat.

The emperor strolled over to the mouse cage holding the bag of food pellets between two of his fingers, waving it back and forth and smiling as he approached. He was acting as if he were bringing some rare treat to his pet instead of the same meal that the mouse had been served every night since his arrival. "Here they co-ome!" sang out Emperor Jon as he lifted the latch and opened the door to the cage. He tossed a handful of food pellets into the cage and started to close the door.

This was the chance that Pie-Rat had been waiting for! He often thought of dashing out of the cage when Jon opened the door to feed him, but he figured that Jon would either catch him or seal the throne room, trapping him inside.

Pie-Rat knew that his plan had to be more subtle, more carefully executed, and now was the time. He took one of the food pellets between his paws and batted it back and forth like a play toy, acting as adorable as possible.

"Aww," cooed Jon. "Isn't that too, too precious? The little mousy-wousy thinks his food is an itsy-bitsy ball. I wish I had my camera!"

If I throw up all over the place, it will blow the whole plan, thought Pie-Rat, trying not to listen. Pie-Rat then maneuvered the pellet over to the side of the door. Just as Emperor Jon started closing the door, Pie-Rat shoved the pellet in between the door and the latch that locked it. Jon closed the door as far as it would go, and, thinking it was secure, turned and walked away from the cage, humming happily to himself.

Pie-Rat glanced at the cage door and saw that his scheme had worked. The tiny pellet was wedged between the door and the latch. The door was still open a crack, but Jon hadn't noticed, partly because his love for the mouse kept him from thinking that the little creature would ever even want to escape, and partly because his general lameness kept him from thinking much of anything.

"Time for the great big emperor to go eat *his* food, wittle mousy," said Jon. "But I'll see you bright and early in the morning! Good night!" Then Jon turned and left the throne room.

At last, thought Pie-Rat. *I have my chance!*

Space Pie-Rat waited until the middle of the night when he was sure that everyone in the palace was sound asleep. Then he pushed open the un-latched cage door and scurried out to freedom. *I'm out!* he thought. *I'm finally out! Okay, Pie-Rat, calm down. What do I do now? How do I get out of this room?*

The mouse scampered across the table on which the cage sat. Coming to the edge, he raced down the table's leg and quickly reached the linoleum floor of the ancient throne room. Scurrying across the floor, he stopped at the bottom of the large oak door that led out of the room. *The crack at the bottom of the door is too small for me to fit through,* he thought. *And even if I could climb up the side of the door and reach the handle, there's no way I could turn it to open the door. I've got to find another way out!*

Pie-Rat dashed back across the room and ran smack into a hard, cold object. *Ouch!* He rubbed his little pink nose with his tiny front paw. *What is this thing?* he wondered. Looking up, he saw that the round, black, metal object bowed out in the middle and had a lip on top that ran around the edge in a circle. *I've got to get a better look at this,* Pie-Rat thought.

The mouse scrambled up to the top of a tall floor lamp that stood next to the object. Balancing on the lampshade, he looked down and realized what the object was. *It's a cauldron! This must be the magic cauldron that the emperor's friend, that freaky sorcerer, uses for his spells. He comes here all the time, and he must have left it on his last visit.*

Pie-Rat peered down into the cauldron's round open mouth. He spotted some liquid that had been left at the bottom. *I wonder if that could be some of the sorcerer's magic brew. What the heck! I've got nothing to lose!*

Space Pie-Rat dove off the table into the cauldron. He hit the liquid with a splash and disappeared beneath its murky surface. Floating back to the top, Pie-Rat felt strange. *I think I'm growing! I feel like I'm getting bigger!*

Indeed he was. Sorcerer Binky's leftover magic brew began to transform the tiny mouse. In a few minutes, Pie-Rat was large enough to stand up and step out of the cauldron. Falling to the cold floor, he felt himself changing, growing larger and larger. Then suddenly, the growing stopped.

Space Pie-Rat got up off the floor and looked at himself in a full-length mirror that hung on the throne room wall. "I'm me again!" he cried, his voice returning with his size. "Only I'm much more than the old me. I'm New, Improved, Giant Economy-Size me!"

Pie-Rat looked like his old self — a large rat with a blue bandanna on his head, topped by a pirate hat (he lost his eye patch in a battle with Pet Force), only now he stood twelve feet tall — twice his previous height!

The towering terror bellowed with rage. "I'm back!" he roared. "And I'm bigger than ever!" He stomped around the room, overcome with relief at finally being out of his cage. He looked into the mirror again and again to make sure his eyes weren't deceiving him. But no, it was true. He really was twelve feet tall.

His astonishment gave way to the fury building up inside him. "I will have my revenge," he snarled to his reflection in the mirror. "And this will help me!" He grabbed a small vial from a shelf and swiftly dunked it into the magic brew. When the vial was full, he capped it. "This brew will give me a weapon against other magic. First, I will find that traitor, Vetvix, and when I am through with her, I will destroy Pet Force!"

3

Space Pie-Rat slowly opened the throne room door. Emperor Jon saw no reason to keep it locked since he believed his beloved pet was secure within his cage. Pie-Rat looked both ways and saw that the hallways were empty. It was the middle of the night and everyone in the palace was fast asleep.

The rejuvenated rodent scurried as quickly and quietly as a twelve-foot-tall creature could. He arrived at the spiral stone stairway that ran through the center of the palace. Bounding on tiptoe from step to step, Pie-Rat made his way down the staircase, arriving at the lowest level of the palace. Gently opening the door at the bottom of the stairwell, he stepped into the palace garage.

"What a junkyard!" Pie-Rat muttered to himself as he peered at the emperor's collection of old vehicles. There sat rusted spaceships that hadn't flown in years, large land-roving vehicles to carry the emperor's army, and individual hovercraft used for skimming just above the planet's surface.

In a corner of the garage Pie-Rat saw some old paint cans, a box of old tools, and a stack of ten-year-old issues of *Monarch's Monthly* magazine. Next to that was the emperor's collection of sale circulars and coupon books from every Sunday newspaper for the last five years. "This guy doesn't throw *anything* out!" Pie-Rat mumbled. Then he came upon Emperor's Jon's personal hovercraft. Peering through the window, he saw a pair of large fuzzy dice hanging from the rearview mirror. "What a nerd!" exclaimed Pie-Rat, shaking his head.

Pie-Rat crossed to the far side of the garage and found what he had been searching for — Pet Force's spaceship, the *Lightspeed Lasagna*! The sleek, state-of-the-art craft had belonged to the original members of Pet Force. When Garfield and his friends were brought into this universe, Emperor Jon gave them the ship to use in their battle against Pie-Rat and Vetvix. The emperor kept the ship in the palace garage in case he ever needed to bring the Earth pets back once again to battle evil as Pet Force.

Space Pie-Rat slipped into the cockpit of the *Lightspeed Lasagna*. He pulled its overhead door shut, conking himself on the head in the process. "Ouch," he yelped, removing his pirate hat and rubbing the sore spot. "I can see there are going to be some drawbacks to being twelve feet tall." Although the ship was designed to hold the five members of Pet Force, none of them was taller than six feet five inches. Pie-Rat's shoulders rounded as he hunched over the control panel of the cramped cockpit.

Space Pie-Rat had flown from one end of the universe to the other during his years as a pirate, smuggler, and all-around bad guy. He had piloted just about every kind of spaceship there was, so it didn't take him long to figure out how to power up the *Lightspeed Lasagna*'s main engines. But he *couldn't* figure out how to open the garage door, which now loomed before him.

"There's nothing on this control panel that can open the stupid door," snarled Pie-Rat, growing annoyed. Then he spied a small, rectangular plastic control stuck to the cockpit ceiling. It was a standard portable garage door opener, held to the ceiling by a piece of Velcro.

Riiip! went the Velcro as Pie-Rat grabbed the opener. "Here it is!" he said triumphantly.

Pie-Rat pointed the opener at the garage door and pressed the button on top. Nothing happened. He pressed it again. Still nothing. "Ahh," he cried. "This must be one of the later models with the security code keypad!"

Sure enough, Pie-Rat flipped over the opener and saw a small numbered keypad on the back. "It could take me weeks to guess the exact four-

number code that will open the door!" he squealed in frustration, tossing the device over his shoulder. He thought for a moment, then smiled an evil smile.

"I don't need that little garage door opener. I have this *great big* garage door opener right here," he said, gesturing to the ship he now commanded.

Pie-Rat put up the *Lightspeed Lasagna*'s front shield to use as a battering ram. Then he fired the ship's rear thrusters and the craft shot forward. The ship crashed right through the garage door, ripping a huge hole in the side of the palace and making a noise that shook the building and woke up everyone inside.

Within seconds, Space Pie-Rat was clear of the planet Polyester's atmosphere and was tearing through the vast reaches of space. The broad expanse of darkness, filled with millions of glowing stars, comforted Pie-Rat.

"Vetvix, Pet Force, your days are numbered!" Pie-Rat cackled as he punched the *Lightspeed Lasagna* into light speed. He sighed a deep sigh and settled back as best he could in the narrow cockpit, plotting his sweet revenge.

4

Emperor Jon was in a deep sleep when the *Lightspeed Lasagna* blasted out of the garage.

The emperor's peaceful slumber was rocked by a terrible sound and jarring jolt that went through the entire palace. He yelled, "Hey! No fair!" and bolted upright in bed, annoyed at the interruption of his beauty sleep. Then he realized that something very bad had just happened.

Emperor Jon slipped on his powder-blue polyester bathrobe with the purple teddy bears on it and dashed from his bedroom. Pandemonium had broken loose in the palace. People were panicked, running in every direction.

The emperor spotted one of his palace guards. "What happened?" he asked.

"Your highness, there seems to have been some kind of an explosion in the palace garage," explained the guard.

"The garage?" cried Jon. "My fuzzy dice are down there! I must go at once!"

Emperor Jon dashed down the spiral stone steps that led from his bedroom on the top floor of the palace to the garage at its lowest level. Around and around he flew down the steps, his fear and anxiety growing with each floor he passed.

Bursting into the garage, Jon ran to his personal hovercraft, peered through the window, and breathed a sigh of relief. "My fuzzy dice are all right!" he gushed. "Thank goodness." Then he turned around and saw that the garage door and the wall surrounding it were gone.

"Oh, no!" cried the emperor as the seriousness of the situation began to dawn on him.

The garage was a blur of activity. The palace guards were investigating the huge hole in the side of the palace and searching for clues.

"What could have caused this?" asked the emperor.

"Your highness, the *Lightspeed Lasagna* is gone," explained one of the guards.

"Gone!" cried Jon. "What do you mean *gone*? It couldn't have just flown off by itself — that's ridiculous! You must be mistaken. Sheesh — who hires the guards around here, anyway?"

"Your highness, we believe that someone *stole* the *Lightspeed Lasagna* and blasted out of the garage with it, causing the huge hole in the wall," the guard said, very slowly and patiently.

"The Pet Force ship has been *stolen*?" muttered the emperor to himself. "Oh. I guess *that* makes sense. But who could have done such a thing? And how did they get into the castle?"

"We don't know, your highness," replied the guard. "The only clue we've found are these huge footprints near the *Lightspeed Lasagna*'s parking space."

Emperor Jon knelt down and examined several enormous footprints. "Whoever or whatever made these prints must be gigantic," he concluded. "How could someone that big sneak into the palace? It's not possible — unless that person was using magic. I need some help. I've got to contact Sorcerer Binky!"

The emperor sent a guard to bring Sorcerer Binky to the palace. A short while later, the two old friends met in Jon's throne room.

"WHAT IS IT YOU REQUIRE, O GREAT EMPEROR, THAT CAUSES YOU TO DRAG ME FROM MY NICE WARM BED IN THE MIDDLE OF THE NIGHT?" asked Sorcerer Binky in his usual incredibly loud voice.

"Uh, the voice, Binky, please," said Emperor Jon, his hands covering his ears.

"YOU WANT ME TO DO THE VOICE-LOWERING SPELL? AT THIS TIME OF THE MORNING?" replied the sorcerer. "YOU

WOULD THINK THAT JUST SHOWING UP
HERE WOULD BE ENOUGH, BUT —"

"Sorcerer Binky!" shouted the emperor, sounding as angry as he ever got.

"I'M SORRY, O KIND AND UNDERSTANDING EMPEROR. I WILL TAKE CARE OF IT AT ONCE!" Sorcerer Binky pulled a long, thin magic wand from his robe and swallowed it in one quick gulp. "How's that?" he asked in a normal voice. The voice-lowering spell had taken effect instantly.

"Much better," replied Jon. "Sorry about the shouting."

"Don't give it another thought, O Forgiving and Patient Ruler," said Sorcerer Binky. "I'm always cranky, too, before I've had my first cauldron of coffee in the morning. Now, what is the problem?"

Emperor Jon filled Sorcerer Binky in on the shocking events that had taken place so far that night.

"I just don't understand how someone that big could have snuck into the palace," said the emperor concluding his story.

"Maybe he didn't have to sneak in," answered Binky as he looked around the throne room. "Look!" He pointed toward the empty mouse cage that had once held Space Pie-Rat. "The mouse has escaped!"

Emperor Jon joined the sorcerer near his cauldron. "You see these mouse-sized footprints?"

asked Binky, pointing to a tiny trail that led from the cage to the cauldron.

"Yes," answered Jon.

"Now look at those huge footprints leading away from the cauldron," continued the sorcerer.

"Those are the same footprints we found in the garage!" exclaimed Jon.

"I believe," began Binky, "that your little pet used my magic brew to change back into Space Pie-Rat — the vicious villain he was before Vetvix cast her evil spell and changed him into a mouse."

"Oh, dear," said Emperor Jon, starting to panic.

"But that's not all," continued Binky, pulling out a tape measure and measuring one of the huge rat footprints. "Based on the size of these footprints, I would calculate that Pie-Rat is now at least twice as big as he used to be — probably around twelve feet tall."

"Twice as big," muttered Jon, fear sweeping through his very being.

"And most likely twice as evil," added the sorcerer. "On top of that, now he's got the *Lightspeed Lasagna* — perhaps the fastest, best-armed ship in the universe."

Emperor Jon slumped back onto his throne, the weight of all this dragging him down. "What will we do?" he asked, his mind racing back to his sweet little pet, then to the image of a twelve-foot-tall Space Pie-Rat, then to his fuzzy dice, then back to Pie-Rat.

"There's only one thing *to* do," replied Sorcerer Binky. "We must bring those five Earth beings back to our universe to become Pet Force once again! Only they can stop Pie-Rat and recover the *Lightspeed Lasagna!*"

5

Our universe, Jon's living room . . .

The driving rain that had started in the early morning hours showed no sign of letting up as the afternoon wore on. This was perfectly fine with Jon Arbuckle, Garfield and Odie's owner. It meant that he could spend the entire day on his living room couch watching his favorite movies on video.

Jon was giggling uncontrollably at *Here Come the Nerds, Part VI*. This was his third *Here Come the Nerds* movie of the day, and, like the rain outside, he showed no sign of letting up. Odie sat curled up next to Jon's feet, staring blankly at the TV screen. The set could have been turned off for all he cared — Odie stared blankly at most things — but he enjoyed hanging out with his friends. He was too dumb to figure out that the toxic smell that had been bothering him all afternoon was coming from Jon's feet, which rested only inches from Odie's nose.

Arlene sat nearby, shifting her attention between the movie and Nermal, who was completely absorbed in reading the latest issue of the *Pet Force* comic book. Arlene kept an eye on Nermal, helping him with any hard words he came across in his reading. Nermal read the *Pet Force* comic with particular interest these days, having actually been through an adventure in Emperor Jon's universe with the others. He constantly wondered whether or not he would ever be called back to serve the emperor as Abnermal, although at the moment, he was lost in the latest story of his comic book heroes.

Garfield, with Pooky by his side, was bored out of his feline skull, as usual. He didn't feel like reading: *All that moving of eye muscles. It's just too close to exercise for my taste.* He didn't feel like watching movies: *What do I have to watch movies about nerds for? I live with Jon.* In fact, he didn't feel like doing much of anything. So for Garfield, it was a pretty typical day, rain or not. He stared at the living room wallpaper, counting the number of strawberries in the pattern against the white background. He finished his third pan of lasagna of the afternoon and was about to dig into his fourth, growing sleepier by the second.

Jon let out a hearty laugh at something one of

the nerds in the movie did. "No matter how many times I see this movie, these guys just *destroy* me!"

Don't I wish, thought Garfield as he shoved a gooey gob of lasagna into his mouth.

Hanging on the wall above the spot where Garfield sat was a framed copy of issue #100 of the *Pet Force* comic. Nermal believed that this special issue, with its embossed, gold-foil, 3-D, holographic, glow-in-the-dark cover — the very cover

that had served as a doorway between universes in the gang's first Pet Force adventure — would be worth big bucks some day. He went way beyond simply putting the issue into a plastic bag as he had done with issues #1 to #99. Issue #100 was proudly displayed behind glass in a gold frame.

"Boy, this is great!" exclaimed Nermal, unable to control his excitement when he got to a full-page battle scene in the current issue. "Just look at this artwork!" He shoved the comic under Garfield's nose.

"Are you going to annoy us all with that ridiculous comic book again?" asked Garfield.

"No," replied Nermal. "Just you!"

"Say, Nermal," began Garfield. "Why don't we not see each other for a while? Like for the rest of our lives!"

Nermal pointed at Garfield's lasagna. "Are you going to eat that?" he asked.

"No," replied Garfield. "I'm going to have it bronzed and put on the mantle. Do you have to be so annoying?"

"Yup," replied Nermal.

Odie was distracted by the bickering between Garfield and Nermal. He trotted over and slobbered on Garfield's pan of lasagna.

"Go chase a parked car, Odie," quipped Garfield.

"Oh, leave him alone," said Arlene, who was also happy for the distraction from the day's boredom.

"But he drooled on my lasagna," whined Garfield.

"Your fourth pan of the day, Moby," Arlene shot back. "Is that your stomach or did you swallow a globe?"

By this time, everyone except Jon had become far more interested in verbally slamming one another than in any of their other rainy-day activities. *This* was fun.

"You know, Arlene," said Garfield. "Your hairdo really suits your face. They're *both* ugly!"

"Oh, yeah?" replied Arlene. "Well, you know what goes best with a face like yours? A paper bag!"

The put-down parade continued. Garfield and his friends were so intent on topping one another that no one noticed when the framed cover of *Pet Force* #100 started to glow. Suddenly, a blinding flash filled the living room.

Jon was doubled over with laughter at the latest nerdish prank in his movie and so he didn't notice the flash. But Garfield, Odie, Arlene, Nermal, and Pooky were pulled into the glowing cover, once again sucked from their universe into the parallel universe to become Pet Force!

6

The parallel universe . . .

Zap! Garfield, Odie, Arlene, Nermal, and Pooky felt themselves sliding through a narrow tunnel filled with brilliant white light. When they stopped moving, the light faded and the image of a room appeared before them. They were sprawled out on the linoleum-covered floor of Emperor Jon's throne room on the planet Polyester.

"Sorry about the cold floor," said Sorcerer Binky, who was standing next to the emperor. "I've got to work on a gentler way to bring you guys here."

"Oh, no, not this again," moaned Garfield. "I didn't even have time to grab some lasagna for the road!" He got up and found himself standing on his back legs. His body was now in the form of the Pet Force leader, Garzooka. At six foot five, he was the tallest of the group. "I was looking forward to

27

a nice afternoon nap that would last for about four afternoons."

One by one, the friends stood up and examined their Pet Force bodies. "Awesome!" exclaimed Nermal, now transformed into Abnermal. "*Being* Pet Force is much cooler than just *reading* about Pet Force!" Then he reached out and froze Garzooka's left arm with his freeze-touch just to get the feel for his powers again. As Abnermal, he also had incredible pester-power, which he liked to use because it really annoyed Garzooka.

Odie was so excited to once again be in the muscular body of Odious that he shot his super-stretchy stun tongue across the room and knocked Abnermal right into a wall. "Thanks, Odious," said Garzooka, whose arm had just about thawed out. "I owe you one."

Odious slobbered his acknowledgment, then stretched out his tongue again. This time it slammed into Garzooka. "I take it back," said the Pet Force leader, shaking off the blow.

Arlene, who had resumed the form of Starlena, was a bit afraid to speak. She recalled that the first time she had received the powers of Starlena, she could not control her hypnotic siren song. Each time she opened her mouth, everyone within earshot fell asleep.

Mustering all her concentration and courage, Starlena spoke. "We are here to serve you, Emperor Jon." Everyone in the room held their breath. Nothing happened. Starlena had not lost the control over her powers that she had learned during her first adventure in the parallel universe. Then, breathing a sigh of relief, she nailed Abnermal — who was still busy pestering Garzooka — with a concentrated siren beam that put him into a stunned trance.

Pooky — now transformed into the hyper-intelligent part-computer, part-teddy bear Compooky — asked the question that was on everyone's mind. "Emperor Jon," he began.

"Something terrible must have happened here in your universe for you to summon us back through the dimensional portal."

"You are right, Compooky," replied Emperor Jon. "Something terrible *has* happened." The emperor proceeded to fill the members of Pet Force in on Space Pie-Rat's extraordinary escape from his mouse cage, his dip in the sorcerer's magic brew, and his transformation into a giant, twelve-foot-tall version of his former self. Pet Force listened in horror as Emperor Jon went on to explain how Pie-Rat had stolen their beloved spaceship, the *Lightspeed Lasagna*, and blasted out of the garage, destroying an entire section of the palace in the bargain.

"So," concluded the emperor, "you must follow Space Pie-Rat and recover the *Lightspeed Lasagna*. And unless I miss my guess —"

That's always a possibility with either Jon in either universe, thought Garzooka.

"— Pie-Rat will lead you to Vetvix," Emperor Jon continued. "She is still somewhere in our universe and has not been heard from since she vanished from her *Orbiting Clinic of Chaos* moments before it blew up. You must confront her once again, as well."

"But Emperor Jon," said Garzooka, stepping forward to assume his role as leader of the team, "how can we follow Space Pie-Rat if he has our ship?"

30

Sorcerer Binky spoke up. "I think I've got the solution. If I may, O Great Emperor?"

"The floor is yours," replied Emperor Jon.

"REALLY!" shouted Sorcerer Binky, his voice returning to its ear-splitting volume in his excitement. "I'VE ALWAYS LOVED THIS LINOLEUM PATTERN! IT'LL LOOK SO GREAT IN MY CASTLE."

Everyone's hands shot to their ears.

"I *meant* that it was your turn to speak," said Emperor Jon, trying hard to keep his patience. He knew that he needed Binky's help if he was to get the stolen ship back.

"Oh," said the disappointed sorcerer, his voice returning to its magically lowered volume. "Well, anyway, to answer your question, Garzooka, my plan is to bring you five to my castle. There, in my basement laboratory, we will combine my magic with Compooky's scientific genius, toss in a little luck, and see if we can build a spaceship in which you, the mighty Pet Force, can go after Pie-Rat."

"But what will we use to build it?" asked Starlena.

"Oh, I've got a few spare parts lying around down there," answered Sorcerer Binky. "I'm sure we'll come up with something."

At that moment, Abnermal — who had been in a trance through the emperor's explanation and the sorcerer's plan — snapped out of it with a start. "What did I miss? What did I miss?" he

31

repeated over and over, jumping on and off Garzooka's back. Garzooka swatted Abnermal across the room with a flick of his super-strong wrist. Then Starlena filled him in on the mission ahead.

"Let's hurry," said Sorcerer Binky as he gestured for Garzooka, Odious, Abnermal, Starlena, and Compooky to follow him. "We've no time to lose."

"Good luck," said Emperor Jon. "Keep me posted on your progress."

"I'll send you an update on c-mail every hour," promised the sorcerer.

"C-mail?" asked the emperor. "Don't you mean *E-mail?*"

"No," replied Binky. "C-mail. Cauldron mail. Every hour a message will appear in the surface of the leftover magic brew in my cauldron here in your throne room. There's no limit to what a good cauldron can do."

Emperor Jon nodded. Then Sorcerer Binky led Pet Force from the palace.

7

Deep within a huge crater, on a moon orbiting a planet not far from Polyester, the evil Vetvix was hard at work. Following the destruction of her *Orbiting Clinic of Chaos*, Vetvix had set up a new base of operations at the bottom of this crater on the otherwise lifeless moon, which she named the *Menacing Moon of Mayhem*. Hidden from view far beneath the moon's surface, Vetvix built an extensive underground hideout and workshop. In her new headquarters, she was hatching her latest evil scheme for domination of Emperor Jon's universe.

"My plan is almost complete," she cackled to her beloved pet, Gorbull. Gorbull was the result of Vetvix's first experiment in combining different animals into powerful mutant creatures. Since that time, Vetvix had manufactured thousands of mutant animals. She controlled these creatures with her magic and telepathic powers, and they served her every whim as obedient soldiers in a bizarre, unnatural army. But Gorbull held a special place in Vetvix's otherwise black heart. He was not a soldier, but rather a spoiled pet. When Vetvix had vanished in a burst of magical smoke just before her *Orbiting Clinic of Chaos* exploded, she had included Gorbull in the spell. She would never try to escape and leave her pet behind.

"Hungry, my pet?" cooed Vetvix. Gorbull immediately sprang to his feet. "I thought so." Vetvix opened her hand and fed Gorbull the gnarly-looking remains of one of her failed experiments. He lapped them up greedily. Then she turned back to her work.

Vetvix stood before a large bank of controls adjusting a series of knobs and levers. Her bodysuit and boots were covered with an animal paw-print design. Metal rings looped around her legs, waist, and arms. Her jet-black hair flowed down her back. On her forehead rested a large headband, in the center of which sat a power crystal — one of the many sources of her evil.

Digital electronic meters flashed on the control panel before her. Vetvix had found a way to combine her magic energy with a powerful electrical charge to create a new variety of mutant creature. She now adjusted the amount of magic electrical energy flowing from the control panel, through a set of thick wires that ran across the floor of her workshop, and into a tall rectangular energization booth.

Before Vetvix could complete her latest experiment, the power suddenly went off. *"No!"* shrieked Vetvix. "How could this happen?"

"Easy," said a familiar voice. "I pulled out the plug."

Vetvix whirled around. There, in the doorway, towering above Vetvix, stood Space Pie-Rat. He now looked exactly like a twelve-foot-tall version of his former self, complete with a new eye patch purchased at the Inter-Galact-O-Mart for $1.99. The unplugged power cord from her latest invention dangled from his huge hand.

"Pie-Rat!" exclaimed Vetvix, trying unsuccessfully to hide her surprise not only at his sudden appearance in her secret base, but also at the fact that her former henchman now stood twelve feet tall. "How did you find me?"

"Your little experiment is sending out an electronic signal from a moon that's supposed to be dead," explained Pie-Rat. "I didn't think anyone was microwaving brownies. I guessed that only one of your foul experiments could be giving off such interesting energy waves."

"It looks like being a mouse has agreed with you," said Vetvix, trying to hide her nervousness. "They've obviously been feeding you well."

"You'll notice I'm not laughing, Vetvix," replied Pie-Rat. "You might have thought it was funny to turn me into a mouse, but let me tell you, spending my days pacing back and forth inside a little cage,

eating cardboard food, and listening to that moronic emperor talk to me like I was a total idiot was not my idea of a good time!"

Every fiber of Vetvix's evil being stood ready. She knew that Pie-Rat had not tracked her down simply for a pleasant chat. She figured that the towering rodent had revenge on his mind and she prepared herself for what would surely be an attack. Vetvix felt confident that her magic could protect her from anything Pie-Rat had planned. What she hadn't counted on was the rodent's plan to fight fire with fire — or in this case, to fight magic with magic.

"I don't suppose you'd care to tell me how you grew so big," said Vetvix slyly.

"As a matter of fact, I'll do better than *tell* you," answered Pie-Rat, reaching into his pocket. "I'll *show* you!"

As Pie-Rat's hand moved for his pocket, the power crystal on Vetvix's headband began to glow. *He's probably got a weapon of some kind in his pocket. I'll just put up a magic force shield from my power crystal to protect myself*, she thought.

Pie-Rat removed his hand from his pocket. What he held in his hand was not a weapon in the typical sense. He clutched the small vial of Sorcerer Binky's magic brew that he had taken from the bottom of the cauldron in Emperor Jon's palace.

"This!" shouted Pie-Rat, opening the vial and

spilling its contents all over Vetvix. "This is what restored me and gave me my new larger body. And this is what will spell your doom!"

A brilliant white glow surrounded Vetvix as the magic brew penetrated her shield. A blinding flash filled the room. Space Pie-Rat looked down and saw that Vetvix, once his master, had been shrunk into a tiny, five-inch-tall version of herself.

Due to its magical properties, only Vetvix's headband containing the power crystal remained its normal size. The headband fell to the floor right next to Vetvix who screamed in a high-pitched voice, "What have you done to me?" as she trembled in terror.

Gorbull growled and slowly approached the teeny tiny being before him. He was confused by her resemblance to Vetvix. He bared his teeth at her, and the mini-Vetvix ran off screeching. Gorbull's instinct took over and the half-gorilla, half-pit bull began chasing his former master — now stripped of her powers as well as her size — around the hideout.

"You'll be sorry, you big hairy beast," Vetvix shouted in her little squeaky voice. "When I'm big again, you'll be very sorry, monkey-breath. I'll make a Gor-burger out of you!" Then she dashed into an open cabinet and pulled the door closed behind her. She opened the door a crack and added, "And I'll deal with you, too, Pie-Rat, you overgrown freak! Just you wait and see!"

Space Pie-Rat ignored Vetvix. He kneeled down and picked up the headband. It didn't fit around his head, so he found a piece of ribbon and attached it to the crystal. *This makes a funky necklace,* he thought to himself. He concentrated with all his might and the magic crystal began to glow. Magic energy crackled from his fingertips.

"Unlimited power is now mine!" he shouted. "Vetvix, you are helpless! I claim your hideout as my own. Only one task remains — the destruction of Pet Force. Then and only then will my revenge truly be complete!"

8

The ancient castle that served as home and laboratory for Sorcerer Binky had fallen into disrepair. The tall stone structure was ramshackle and filled with junk. The inside looked like a cross between a flea market and a used-car lot. Pieces of vehicles, parts of old buildings, and collections of stuff — all kinds of stuff — filled the castle.

None of this bothered Sorcerer Binky. His active mind was filled with loftier ideas. Magic spells, ancient potions, and old chili recipes filled his cluttered brain the way piles of age-old junk filled his home.

In the basement laboratory of the stone castle, the sorcerer was hard at work with the members of Pet Force, trying to assemble a space vehicle from the bits and pieces he had lying around.

"The body is almost finished," announced Sorcerer Binky. He had pieced a spaceship hull together out of sections salvaged from spaceships that had crashed into the planet Polyester over the years, as well as some aluminum siding left over from a renovation job that Binky had helped Emperor Jon with at the emperor's palace a few years earlier.

"I know I've got the perfect thing to use as a control panel around here somewhere," the sorcerer continued. "It's the dashboard from a 1957 Buick. A real classic!" He was bent over, waist deep in a huge box of old junk, tossing smashed-up toasters, ripped shoes, rusty cauldrons, and broken magic wands over his shoulder as he searched for the dashboard.

"You've got everything in there but the kitchen sink," commented Starlena.

"Ah, here it is!" shouted Binky triumphantly.

"What, the dashboard?" asked Garzooka.

"No, the kitchen sink!" replied the sorcerer. "I knew it was around here somewhere."

Binky's search for the dashboard led him to the castle's attic. He flung open the heavy door and hundreds of bats flew out, swarming all over the castle. "Don't mind them," Binky called down to the members of Pet Force who were waiting below in the laboratory. "They came with the castle."

The sound of large items being thrown around the attic and crashing to the floor echoed throughout the castle. Finally Sorcerer Binky shouted, "I found it! I've got the dashboard!"

Racing downstairs, Binky got to work installing

the dashboard as a control panel for the makeshift vessel.

Meanwhile, Compooky had already designed the ship's main computer system from circuits, chips, and old wiring that the sorcerer had lying around. "Garzooka, I'm finished with the guidance system," reported Compooky. "It's ready to be wired into the ship's main computer, but I'm afraid that even with my hyper-intelligent brain, it will take quite a while to connect each of the hundreds of wires to the correct locations on the main computer."

"Not to worry!" said Sorcerer Binky cheerily. "I'll just whip up a quick spell that will make all the wires move instantly to their proper connections. Watch!"

The sorcerer threw open an old wooden trunk. After tossing out another heap of junk — including a variety of pointy hats, old robes, and a bunch of outdated copies of *Wizard's Weekly* magazine — he pulled out a tiny, five-inch-wide, iron cauldron from the bottom of the trunk.

"What a tiny cauldron," observed Starlena.

"Yes, well, a *little* magic goes a long way," replied Sorcerer Binky.

"Now let's see . . ." Binky reached into his cabinet of magic ingredients. "A little magic broth to start with," he said, pouring a small amount of red, bubbly liquid into the cauldron. "Then a teaspoon of ground-up raven's teeth, a pinch of dried snakeskin, and two tablespoons of oregano. Stir briskly and *poof*!"

A thin line of red smoke drifted up out of the little cauldron and moved over to the ship, where Compooky had placed the guidance unit next to the main computer. The magic smoke hit the wires and the tangled mess sprang to life. One by one the wires leading from the guidance system moved by themselves, each one snaking through the dashboard to find its home in the ship's main computer.

"It's working!" yelled the sorcerer.

Then something strange happened. The hundreds of wires all began to change — into strands of spaghetti! Within seconds, the plastic-coated copper wires had become a wiggling mass of stringy pasta.

"That reminds me," said Garzooka. "I'm starving!" Greedily, he grabbed the writhing spaghetti strands and ate every last one.

"Nice going, Mr. Bottomless-Pit-for-a-Stomach!" snapped Abnermal. "You just ate part of our guidance system."

"What are we supposed to do now?" added Starlena. "Consult your stomach for landing coordinates?"

"You're just jealous that I got there first," replied Garzooka, letting out a small, satisfied burp.

"Sorry about that," said Sorcerer Binky. "I

must have used too much oregano! Let me try again."

This time the sorcerer changed his spell a bit. The wires formed again and connected themselves with no problem. The combination of magic and technology would have to work if this spaceship was ever going to get off the ground.

Piece by piece, the ship slowly came together. Seats were made from old cushions and strengthened with a bit of magic fabric. Compooky repaired some old handheld lasers and Binky enlarged and installed them magically, giving the ship a working weapons system. A large cauldron filled with a powerful batch of magic brew sat at the center of the ship's engines, which had been built by Compooky. Finally the ship was ready. "Let's power it up," said Abnermal, jumping around impatiently.

"I think it needs a name first," suggested Sorcerer Binky.

Garzooka stepped forward. "I christen this spaceship the *Planetary Pizza*!" he said. Then he took a jar of tomato sauce and smashed it against the hull.

The five members of Pet Force scrambled inside.

"Hey, your elbow is right in my face, Garzooka," complained Abnermal when the crew had settled into their cramped quarters.

44

"Move your cape, it's wrapped around my neck!" Garzooka complained right back at him.

Odious opened his mouth and the walls of the cockpit were instantly covered with drool.

"Are you ready to fire up the engines?" asked the sorcerer from outside the ship.

"If we don't kill each other first, we'll be fine!" said Starlena.

"Main engine power-up," announced Compooky as the others cleaned up the drool. Then he inserted the key and turned the ignition on the beautiful Buick dashboard.

The magic brew at the center of the ship bubbled furiously. The engines roared to life, and before they knew it, Pet Force had blasted off from Sorcerer Binky's castle. The *Planetary Pizza* was off on its first mission, in hot pursuit of the *Lightspeed Lasagna*.

"I guess we should have moved the ship outside first," Sorcerer Binky muttered to himself. He sighed and looked up at the huge hole the ship had just ripped in his ceiling.

9

The *Planetary Pizza* cut through the inky blackness of space. Inside its cramped cockpit, the five members of Pet Force were growing crankier by the minute.

"There's nothing like a ride in a makeshift, rattling, half-magic, half-used car that's too small for three — much less five — to make you appreciate the *Lightspeed Lasagna!*" complained Garzooka.

"Well, if you weren't so huge, maybe there'd be room for someone else!" replied Abnermal.

"And if you two stopped arguing and whining then maybe we could all have a slightly more pleasant trip!" shot back Starlena. "Look, we'd all like to have our own ship back, but a nasty bad guy took it. That's why we built this ship. So we can get the *Lightspeed Lasagna* back. Remember?"

Starlena banged her fist on the arm of her chair to help make her point and a panel in the ceiling just above her head fell out. Abnermal reacted quickly, throwing up his force shield. The panel bounced harmlessly off the shield.

"Great," said Garzooka sarcastically. "Now we have to use our superpowers to protect ourselves from our own ship!"

Odious yawned, and his super-stretchy stun tongue shot around the tiny cabin like a pinball in a pinball machine. *Ping! Ping! Ping!* went his tongue as it struck and rendered Garzooka, Starlena, and Abnermal senseless.

The muscle-bound mutt stared at his dazed teammates with a puzzled expression on his face. Then he stretched out his titanic tongue and stunned himself on the top of the head, joining his friends in a blissful sleep. Compooky said nothing. The *Planetary Pizza* proceeded on its course — searching out the *Lightspeed Lasagna* — in silence for the first time since the mission began, its unconscious crew sprawled all over one another.

A blaring alarm shrieked a short time later, rousing Pet Force back to their senses. After they each gave Odious a dirty look, the superheroes checked out their stations.

"Thank goodness his tongue was set for 'stun' and not 'total mental meltdown,'" muttered Abnermal.

Compooky looked at his sensor readings. "The automatic sensors picked up the energy readings of the *Lightspeed Lasagna* while you were all unconscious and sounded the alarm," he explained, switching off the bleating noise. "We must be close to the path Space Pie-Rat took when he fled with our ship."

"I'll check it out on my viewscreen," said Starlena. She pushed a button on the control panel before her and a round glass screen — made from an old mirror Sorcerer Binky found in his castle — popped up. Starlena flipped on the viewscreen's power and the circular screen instantly turned into a large pepperoni pizza. Binky's magic had struck again.

"I take back any bad things I might have said about this ship," said Garzooka, grabbing the pizza and opening his mouth wide.

"No, Garzooka! Wait!" shouted Starlena.

But it was too late. The Pet Force leader shoved the entire pizza into his gaping mouth and gobbled it down in a single swallow.

"Nice going, Jaws," said Starlena disgustedly. "Always thinking with your stomach. Now what are we going to use for a viewscreen?"

Compooky came drifting over to Starlena's station. "I can plug my personal monitor into the sensor system," he explained. Compooky had a small monitor that rested on top of his head. He now connected it to Starlena's sensor port.

The image of an energy trail formed on the monitor. "According to these readings," said Compooky, "this trail definitely belongs to the *Lightspeed Lasagna*."

"Increase speed, Abnermal," ordered Garzooka.

Abnermal pushed the *Planetary Pizza*'s engines to maximum power. The small, homemade ship shot off in a burst of speed, hot on the trail of the *Lightspeed Lasagna*.

The energy trail led Pet Force to a small moon that loomed in the distance. "My readings indicate that the trail ends at that moon," reported Compooky.

"It's a safe bet that Vetvix has set up her new base on that moon," said Starlena. "I bet that's where we'll find the *Lightspeed Lasagna*."

"Actually, Starlena," Compooky said, "I believe that Vetvix's base is not *on* that moon, but rather *in* the moon. The energy readings disappear into a huge crater. I believe we'll find our missing ship at the bottom of it."

"Good work, team," complimented Garzooka. "Let's move in, but very carefully."

Suddenly the *Planetary Pizza*'s communication system began to beep.

"Incoming message from Emperor Jon," announced Compooky.

Garzooka flipped on his speaker and Emperor Jon's voice came through muffled by static.

"Garzooka," the emperor greeted him. "I'm checking in for a status report."

"I didn't think you were calling to say happy birthday," replied Garzooka.

"I didn't know it was your birthday," said Emperor Jon.

"It's not," explained Garzooka. "That was just a little joke . . . never mind." Garzooka rolled his eyes. "We've had a little trouble with the ship, but our sensors have picked up a signal from the *Lightspeed Lasagna*. We think we've found Pie-Rat, and probably Vetvix, too."

"Nice work, Pet Force," replied Jon. "I'm losing your signal so I'll sign off for now. Keep me posted. Emperor Jon out. Oh, and happy birthday, Garzooka." Then the static-filled transmission ended.

When Vetvix set up her hidden base deep within the moon's crater, she didn't bother with any defensive systems, figuring that the base was so well hidden that no one would ever find it. This had enabled Pie-Rat to easily land the *Lightspeed*

Lasagna, and now allowed Pet Force to do the same with the *Planetary Pizza.*

The five heroes stepped from the ship and burst into the hideout. They found themselves face-to-face with Space Pie-Rat — all twelve feet of him — wearing Vetvix's power crystal.

"Well, isn't this convenient?" said Pie-Rat chuckling to himself. "Here I was wondering how I could track down the powerful Pet Force and destroy you, when you save me the trouble by walking right through my front door. How do you like my new hideout? If I had known you were coming, I'd have put out some chips and dips. Actually," he continued, gesturing at Pet Force, "it looks like the dips are here!"

"Where's our ship, funny guy?" snarled Garzooka. "And how did you get so big? And how did you put together a base like this so quickly? And where's Vetvix?"

"So many questions, so little time," replied Pie-Rat. "But I'm a nice guy, so I'll answer them. My new, improved size came from a bath in your sorcerer's cauldron. Vetvix built this hideout, but at the moment she's a little busy. In fact, she's a very, very little busy."

At that moment, the five-inch-tall Vetvix scurried past the feet of Pet Force. A growling, snarling Gorbull was still hot on her heels. Garzooka and the others looked down in stunned amazement at the once-threatening villain, now reduced to a walking, talking doll.

"Just you wait until I'm big again, Pet Pinheads," squeaked Vetvix. "I'll get you. And my little dog, too!"

"As for your ship," continued Pie-Rat when Vetvix and Gorbull had disappeared from sight. "I borrowed it to escape from that annoying emperor. But don't worry — you won't be needing it anymore. As a matter of fact, you won't be needing much of anything anymore, because it is time for you to meet your doom!"

10

The power crystal that Pie-Rat wore as a necklace began to glow a sickly green. Energy waves shot from the crystal, radiating in all directions and knocking Pet Force off their feet.

Starlena countered with her hypnotic siren song. "Name this tune, Pie-Rat!" she shouted, then blurted out a high-pitched note, directing it right at Pie-Rat.

Pie-Rat reacted quickly, firing a magic spell from the crystal that met the siren song head on, creating hundreds of tiny musical notes that fell to the ground, then turned and scurried toward Starlena.

"This is too weird," said Starlena as the little army of quarter notes, half notes, and whole notes advanced menacingly, baring sharp pin-like teeth.

Odious reacted quickly, striking each tiny walking note with his super-stretchy stun tongue. The magically created notes disintegrated upon contact with Odious's tongue.

Pie-Rat moved to a wall of cages that held small animals — mice, rats, gerbils, hamsters — that Vetvix would have turned into monsters. "Let's even up the sides a bit," he quipped, flinging open the cage doors, then casting a spell from the crystal.

The various harmless rodents quickly turned into vicious troll-like creatures with pointy teeth and long, sharp claws. The hideous creatures scurried toward Pet Force.

Two trolls leaped right at Garzooka's head. "I've got you covered!" shouted Abnermal, putting up his force shield just in time. The trolls bounced harmlessly away.

Then Abnermal turned and fired a freeze blast at Pie-Rat. The enormous rodent met the blast with a magic spell that caused a mini-blizzard to break out in the hideout. Whipping winds and blinding snow covered everything.

Compooky plugged into the hideout's climate control system and raised the temperature to melt the snow just as two trolls jumped onto his back. Odious leaped across the room, peeled the trolls off, and flung them right at Pie-Rat like a pitcher tossing two fastballs.

Pie-Rat reacted instinctively to the flying objects hurling toward him and protected himself with a magic energy shield that fried the trolls when they smashed into it. "Enough fun and games!" snarled an angry Pie-Rat.

Pie-Rat's enormous body was now completely

surrounded by a magic green glow that gave him incredible strength. A heavy lab table stood between him and Pet Force. He tossed it aside as if it were a piece of paper and charged at the heroes.

Starlena was knocked unconscious with one powerful punch. Compooky was batted out of the air and crash-landed in a corner. Even Abnermal's force shield could not withstand the strength of Pie-Rat's magically enhanced fist, and he, too, went down.

Odious and Garzooka, the two strongest members of Pet Force, teamed up and tackled Pie-Rat together.

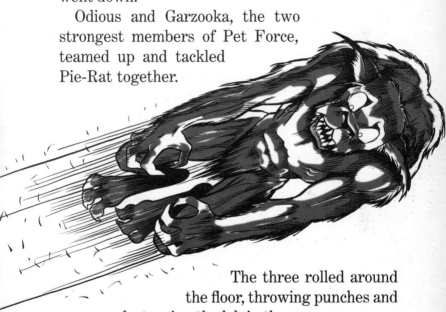

The three rolled around the floor, throwing punches and destroying the lab in the process.

Odious fired his stun tongue at Pie-Rat, but thanks to the magic crystal, the giant rodent was too quick. He grabbed Odious's tongue and stuffed it back into the hero's mouth, delivering a potent punch in the bargain. Odious reeled backward and smashed into a wall across the room.

"So it's you and me now, Garzooka!" said Pie-Rat, slamming Garzooka to the ground. "Just the two of us."

"Well, at least all this magic hasn't taken away your ability to count!" snapped back Garzooka.

Pie-Rat had the Pet Force leader pinned to the ground. One hand held Garzooka's shoulders and the other was slowly aiming the power crystal — right at Garzooka! Struggle as he might, Garzooka could not match Pie-Rat's magical strength.

"And now I will destroy you and the rest of Pet Force!" cackled Pie-Rat gleefully as the crystal began to glow.

Garzooka had time for one last desperate move. He fired a gamma-radiated hairball at Pie-Rat at pointblank range. A powerful explosion filled the room. Although Pie-Rat's magic shield protected him from the blast, the explosion was enough to act as a distraction.

"A useless gesture!" shouted Pie-Rat, but he released his grip on Garzooka's shoulder for a split second. That was all the time the Pet Force leader needed. Garzooka freed his right arm and slashed at Pie-Rat's necklace with his razor-sharp claw. He sliced through the ribbon with one swift motion, then caught the falling necklace and power crystal and slipped them into his pocket.

"Let's see how you do without the magic power crystal, Pie-Rat," said Garzooka as he gave the villain a powerful punch that sent him reeling. Pie-Rat crumpled in a heap.

Garzooka quickly checked on his friends, who were all still shaken up, but not badly hurt. Then he pulled the necklace from his pocket. "And to think that so much trouble could have been caused by this little crystal," he said, tying the cut ends of the necklace together. "I wonder . . ."

And now it became clear that the magic crystal *had* affected Garzooka's brain when Pie-Rat aimed it at him. Garzooka — who never would have done anything so foolish if he were in his right mind — was overcome with the urge to put on the necklace. He slipped it over his head.

The crystal in the necklace began to glow with an eerie red light and Garzooka underwent a frightening transformation. His fur stood on end. A strange glimmer appeared in his eyes. An evil smile spread across his face and Garzooka roared with a sickening laugh.

"I guess I've been wasting my time hanging out with you do-gooders," he announced. "Evil is much more fun. I can see that now!"

"Garzooka, take that thing off," ordered Starlena. "It's warping your mind and turning you evil!" She reached up for the crystal, but Garzooka shoved her arm away.

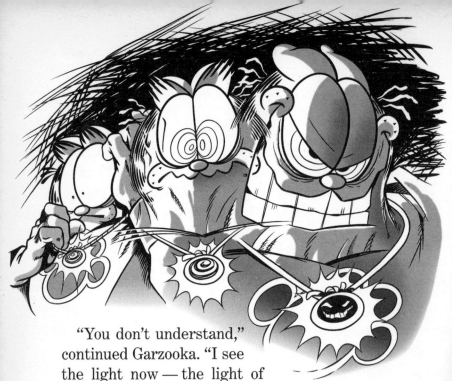

"You don't understand," continued Garzooka. "I see the light now — the light of evil. I will use my awesome power to take what I want. I'll take food, I'll take naps, and food, and more naps, and did I mention food?"

Pet Force was stunned. Compooky floated over to Garzooka and tried to reason with him. "Your actions are quite irrational, Garzooka," Compooky pleaded. "I believe that once you remove that power crystal, you will return to normal."

"But I don't want to return to normal!" Garzooka shouted, slapping Compooky away.

"That's it!" cried Abnermal. "Time to get tough." He fired a freeze blast at Garzooka, but the Pet Force leader easily blocked it with a shield projected from the crystal.

Starlena aimed a concentrated siren song right at Garzooka's ears, but as usual, he was immune to its power.

Odious was their last hope. He jumped on Garzooka, and the two wrestled for a few minutes. "Even without this power crystal, you're no match for my strength, slobber-brain," said Garzooka, getting the upper hand. "But as long as I *do* have the power crystal, you're dog meat!" Garzooka lifted Odious over his head and tossed the stunned canine away.

"Now, let's go have some fun in my ship!" shouted Garzooka.

Pie-Rat was still dazed from the blow Garzooka had dealt him only minutes earlier. It took him a few seconds to realize that Garzooka was talking to *him*.

"Me?" asked a startled Pie-Rat.

"Come on, buddy," said Garzooka, taking Pie-Rat by the arm. "I was all wrong about you and this whole evil thing. Let's go!"

"It's good to have my old ship back," sighed Garzooka as he and Space Pie-Rat settled into the *Lightspeed Lasagna* and took off for a destructive joy ride of evil.

11

The remaining Pet Force members were left to gather their wits — a fairly easy task for all except Odious — after Garzooka's departure.

"I can't believe he's turned to evil," said Abnermal. "He was obnoxious enough the way he was!"

Starlena used the *Planetary Pizza*'s communication system to contact Emperor Jon. He placed her in temporary command of Pet Force.

"What a terrible thing to have happened to Garzooka," said the emperor, his voice once again drifting through the static. "And on his birthday, too! You must take the *Planetary Pizza* and stop him at all costs." Emperor Jon signed off.

"Starlena, wouldn't this be a good time to capture Vetvix?" asked Compooky. "Her tiny size and lack of power seems to make her an easy target."

"As nice as that would be, I don't think we've got the time, now that she's run off," replied Starlena. "She's so tiny that it could take hours just to find her in this complex, and those are hours we just don't have. There's no telling what damage Garzooka and Pie-Rat could do in that time. No, our mission is clear. We must follow the *Lightspeed Lasagna* and free Garzooka from the evil spell that enslaves him."

On board the *Lightspeed Lasagna*, the now-evil Garzooka and his new buddy Space Pie-Rat were getting along famously.

"What an incredible feeling of power!" roared Garzooka as the ship tore through space. "No sense of responsibility. No guilt to always do the right thing. And no pain-in-the-neck teammates to boss me around. I love being bad!"

"What did I tell you, pal?" replied Pie-Rat. "Being evil means you never have to say you're sorry. Or *please*, or *thank you*, or *you're welcome*, or *no problem*. It means doing whatever you feel like."

"Well, what I feel like doing now is —"

"No, wait!" interrupted Pie-Rat. "Let me guess. What you feel like doing now is eating!"

"How'd you know?" exclaimed Garzooka, laughing evilly.

"I know just the place," said Pie-Rat. "It's a food storage planet called Deli not far from here. We swoop in, you use your incredible superpowers to raid the place, and *bingo*! It's Snack City for the greatest criminal duo in history. Space Pie-Rat and Gar —"

63

"Hey!" shouted Garzooka. "Who's the one with the superpowers and the really cool spaceship, anyway?"

"You're right, you're right," conceded Pie-Rat. "The criminal duo of Garzooka and Pie-Rat rules!"

A short while later a small planet came into view.

"There," cried Pie-Rat. "Deli. Home of many, many tasty treats. Let's show them exactly who they're dealing with!"

Garzooka piloted the *Lightspeed Lasagna* down toward the planet's surface. As he approached, he spotted warehouses lined up as far as the eye could see. Each warehouse had several guards in front. They were no match for the *Lightspeed Lasagna*.

The swift spaceship swooped low, firing its laser cannons left and right. Guards jumped out of the way of the blasts as the laser fire ripped open the front of a warehouse. Then Garzooka landed the *Lightspeed Lasagna* and the two villainous partners leaped from the ship.

"Halt!" shouted a guard.

"I don't think so," replied Garzooka. He fired a gamma-radiated hairball at the guard. The hairball struck the guard's laser rifle, which melted like taffy in his hands. The guard dove at Garzooka's midsection, but the powerful former hero brushed him away with a casual swipe.

"You start in on the food, Pie-Rat," ordered Garzooka. "I'll take care of these other guards." As Space Pie-Rat loaded crate after crate of food into the *Lightspeed Lasagna*, Garzooka prepared to battle the guards that now rushed toward him.

Using his speed to dodge their laser blasts, Garzooka used his razor-sharp claw to slice through some weapons, melting others simultaneously with his high-powered hairballs. Most of the guards fled in terror. Those brave or foolish enough to challenge Garzooka were soon unconscious, felled by blows from his powerful, hairy paws.

The duo struck like a tornado and left just as quickly. Within minutes, Pie-Rat had filled the ship with food, and the *Lightspeed Lasagna* blasted back into space.

"It's snack time!" shouted Pie-Rat, ripping the top off a case of soda once the planet Deli had faded back into the blackness of space. Pie-Rat popped open two super-sugared, double-fizz colas, and handed one to Garzooka. "A toast," said the huge rat. "To our newfound partnership of evil."

"A toast," repeated Garzooka, clinking cans and taking a long sip. "And speaking of toast, I'm starving!" The partners hungrily dug into their stash of stolen food.

*　　*　　*

The remaining members of Pet Force, led by Starlena, zoomed along in the *Planetary Pizza.* They had lost track of the faster *Lightspeed Lasagna,* but the time it took Garzooka and Pie-Rat to stage their raid of the planet Deli allowed Starlena and the others to catch up.

As the *Lightspeed Lasagna* came back into view, Odious began pacing back and forth along the length of the ship, slobbering and worrying, worrying and slobbering.

"Please sit down, Odious," said Starlena. "You're making me nervous and you're getting everything wet."

Odious stopped and sat. He continued his worrying and slobbering in place.

"I'm worried, too," Starlena continued. "We've got to find a way to slow down the *Lightspeed Lasagna* so we can board it. If we can do that, we've still got to figure out how to remove the magic power crystal and change Garzooka back from evil to good."

"I don't know," said Abnermal. "I kind of like him evil. At least it gives him a personality."

Starlena glared at her teammate.

"Kidding!" said Abnermal, throwing up his hands. "Just kidding. You know, breaking the tension, that sort of thing. Never mind!"

"Starlena, I think I may have found a way to slow them down a bit," announced Compooky as he crawled under the ship's dashboard and pulled out the container of Binky's magic brew. "Perhaps we can use this ship's magic to our advantage for once. We know the secret code that controls the *Lightspeed Lasagna*'s main power systems. If we can fire a magic energy signal at the *Lasagna* that contains the secret code, we can order the *Lasagna*'s power systems to shut down. Then we can board the ship."

"We'll have to make up the rest as we go along," replied Starlena. "But I like your idea. Can you do it?"

"I have been studying the ways the magic elements of this ship interact with the electrical ones," answered Compooky. "I believe I can do this."

"Then get busy, Compooky," ordered Starlena. "Abnermal, see if you can get any more speed out of this ship. I'd like to be as close as possible when we fire the magic energy signal." Then she leaned back in her seat and thought of the battle to come.

Back on the *Lightspeed Lasagna*, the cockpit of the ship was littered with empty pizza boxes, ice cream containers, and pie tins taken from the raid on the planet Deli.

"Are there any more fries, Pie-Rat?" asked Garzooka as he stuffed three burgers into his face. "I think I have a little bit of room left in my mouth!"

"Sure," replied Pie-Rat, grabbing a fistful of fries from their cardboard container and tossing them into the air like long, stringy free throws heading for Garzooka's open mouth. The fries bounced off Garzooka's face, and the two evil friends broke into gales of laughter.

"How about another dessert?" Garzooka asked. "You've only had seven this morning!" Then he grabbed a long chocolate eclair and slam-dunked it into Pie-Rat's mouth, mushing the gooey treat all over the rodent's face. Again, they fell all over each other in fits of hysterics.

"This is so much more fun than hanging around with those Pet Force do-good losers," said Garzooka as he emptied the remainder of the fries into his mouth. "They always got on my nerves — especially that Abnermal. Whining in that little mousy — nothing personal, Pie-Rat — voice, always complaining and pestering me. 'When are we going to be there, Garzooka?' 'How many bad guys are there going to be, Garzooka?' 'Look, I froze your tail just to be annoying, Garzooka!'"

"And what about that Starlena?" Pie-Rat asked. "She thinks she's so great, singing that stupid song of hers. She couldn't carry a tune if you gave her a bucket."

"And she's soooo serious all the time," added Garzooka. "No fun at all."

"Odious," continued Pie-Rat. "He's so dumb he'd sleep with the windows open in a submarine!"

Garzooka roared with laughter. "Yeah, he's so dumb a mind reader would only charge him half price!"

68

"I think he left his brain to science and they made an early withdrawal," added Pie-Rat. Tears were pouring down Garzooka's face from laughing so hard.

"And Compooky," began Garzooka. "He thinks he's so smart. Always got the answer, always got the analysis, always trying to show me up, challenge my leadership. And all he is, really, is the world's cutest teddy bear."

Garzooka's face went blank. *World's cutest teddy bear, world's cutest teddy bear...* The phrase echoed in the deepest recesses of Garzooka's mind, touching some buried part of his brain.

"Hey! What's the matter, Garzooka?" asked Pie-Rat. "You look like you've seen a ghost."

Garzooka shook his head to clear the cobwebs from his brain. "No, no, it's nothing. I'm fine. Is there any more cake left?" He grabbed half a chocolate cake and devoured it in three bites.

Suddenly all the power on the *Lightspeed Lasagna* went off. The ship stopped dead in space.

"What's going on?" asked Pie-Rat.

Garzooka glanced out the window and saw the *Planetary Pizza*.

"Prepare for battle, Pie-Rat," he snarled.

*   *   *

"Nice work, Compooky!" exclaimed Starlena. "That coded magic energy signal stopped them cold."

Starlena piloted the *Planetary Pizza* into a docking port on the *Lightspeed Lasagna*. "Be careful, Pet Force," she warned. "We must be ready for anything."

Odious shook his head and slobbered as if to say *I'm always ready for anything. It's one of the advantages of never having any thoughts.*

"Garzooka's about to get a *cold* reception," said Abnermal, bracing himself.

Starlena pressed the controls to open the door leading into the *Lightspeed Lasagna*, but nothing happened. Garzooka had sealed it shut. "Odious, see if you can open that door," Starlena ordered.

Odious trotted over to the door and pressed the same control switch that Starlena had just tried. Not surprisingly, nothing happened once again.

"No, Odious," said Starlena as patiently as she could despite her nervousness at the coming confrontation. "Use your muscles." She flexed her own muscle and pointed at her arm. Odious seemed to get the idea.

Odious grabbed the docking port door, took a deep breath, then ripped the door off its hinges, tossing it into the *Lightspeed Lasagna*.

Pet Force burst into the *Lightspeed Lasagna* and found themselves face-to-face with Garzooka and Space Pie-Rat.

12

"**T**his madness must stop now, Garzooka!" shouted Starlena. "You must be restored as the rightful leader of Pet Force!"

"Didn't I tell you, Pie-Rat?" said Garzooka. "She's always soooo serious!"

"Now! Odious!" ordered Starlena.

Odious pounced on Space Pie-Rat, knocking him to the ground. Despite Pie-Rat's twelve-foot-size Odious easily overpowered him with his stupendous superior strength. Without the magic crystal, the rodent villain was no match for the dynamic dog of do-gooding. Odious pinned Pie-Rat's shoulders to the floor, his bulging biceps bursting with power. He then struck with his super-stretchy stun tongue, scrambling Pie-Rat's brain.

Starlena had hoped to reason with Garzooka, but he would have no part of her plan. "Just take that crystal off and come back to us," Starlena begged. "It's that easy!"

"I've had about enough of your whining," replied Garzooka. He moved menacingly toward her.

Starlena tried to sing her siren song, aimed precisely right in Garzooka's face. The shrill melody drifted right past Garzooka with no effect. It did, however, cause Odious to fall into a blissful, but very brief, trance and collapse on top of Pie-Rat, knocking the rodent unconscious.

"Did you forget that your siren song has no effect on me?" asked Garzooka as he jumped toward Starlena.

Abnermal fired a freeze blast at the metal floor in front of Garzooka. A thin sheet of ice spread out before him. Garzooka slid right past Starlena and crashed into a wall. The noise was enough to wake Odious from his trance. "Nice move, big guy," quipped Abnermal. "It's only a couple of years until the next Olympics. I think you'll need to work on your landing, but your short program is a knockout!"

Garzooka was stunned just long enough for Odious to pounce on top of him. The two wrestled around the cabin of the *Lightspeed Lasagna*, their powerful muscles bulging with the strain of battle. Just as Odious appeared to have the advantage, Garzooka shook him off.

"Heel, doggie!" shouted Garzooka as he fired a magic energy ray from the power crystal. Odious immediately began crawling around on all fours, sniffing the floor and whimpering like a frightened puppy.

Before Abnermal could fire another freeze blast, Garzooka cast another magic spell. Abnermal turned into a large ice cube and immediately began to melt all over the ship's floor.

At that moment, Odious's stun blast wore off and Pie-Rat recovered his senses. He grabbed Compooky by the head. "Okay, Pet Force, stop where you are," shouted Pie-Rat. "Give up or I'll twist the little teddy's head off."

The ever-resourceful Compooky sent a small electrical jolt from his circuits into Pie-Rat's hands. "Yow!" yelped Pie-Rat, stung by the shock. Starlena sang out with her siren song, and the huge rat fell into a daze again.

Garzooka sprang suddenly, knocking Starlena to the ground. "Enough," he snarled. "It was cute for a while, but this ends now." His left hand tightened in a death grip around her neck. His right hand, with razor-sharp claw fully extended, raised above his head. He was about to bring his claw down with one swift determined motion and slice his former teammate to shreds.

Starlena, barely able to breathe from the hand that encased her windpipe, decided that she had one last desperate chance to make contact with the part of Garzooka that was still good — or at least, still Garfield. A good, old-fashioned Arlene insult was her only hope.

She stared deeply into Garzooka's eyes and said, "Would you mind turning your face away before you kill me? Your breath smells like you swallowed Jon's dirty sweat socks!"

Somewhere, deep in the back of Garzooka's brain, past the evil influence of the power crystal, past the point where Garfield ended and Garzooka began, and just to the left of a large glob of mozzarella cheese, a small glint of recognition registered, causing him to hesitate for just a moment.

Starlena took full advantage of this moment. She grabbed Garzooka's right arm and used his own razor-sharp claw to

slice the evil crystal necklace that hung from his neck. The necklace fell to the floor, shattering the crystal into numerous tiny shards. Garzooka shook his head, then looked down at Starlena.

"I'm free from that evil spell," he proclaimed. "I'm myself again. Starlena, thank you. How can I ever repay you?"

"You could start by taking your hand off my windpipe," she replied in a weak, choked voice. "If it's not too much trouble."

"Listen, Starlena," said Garzooka when he had released her. "I'm sorry about what I said back there."

"Don't worry about it," replied Starlena. "You don't need an evil power crystal to insult me. You do just fine on your own. Oh, and that thing I said about your breath smelling like Jon's socks? That's true."

The instant that the power crystal shattered, its magic effects were reversed. Odious stood up on his back legs and stopped whimpering. The spreading puddle of water that was Abnermal returned to his superhero body. "Boy, I'm glad no one wanted a cold drink," he said, feeling his body to make sure it was all still there.

Odious trotted over and slobbered a welcome-back greeting all over Garzooka. Then the two of them placed the still-unconscious Space Pie-Rat into the largest prison cell aboard the ship — one that would hold the villain's twelve-foot frame.

Then, with the *Planetary Pizza* still docked, Garzooka took command of the *Lightspeed Lasagna*. "We've got to go back to the planet Deli and set everything straight," explained Garzooka. "Pie-Rat and I made quite a mess of things there. But first we've got to get back to the *Menacing Moon of Mayhem* and capture Vetvix!"

Compooky was able to restore power to the *Lightspeed Lasagna* within a couple of hours, and the reunited Pet Force sped off toward the *Menacing Moon of Mayhem*.

Late that night, while Pet Force slept and the *Lightspeed Lasagna* proceeded on automatic pilot, Sorcerer Binky's magic brew finally wore off Space Pie-Rat. The strange concoction that had restored Pie-Rat and enlarged him to his twelve-foot height finally ran out of magic power. Pie-Rat returned to his normal, six-foot-tall size. The transformation startled him. At first he was upset that he was no longer huge, but then he spotted one immediate advantage.

Pie-Rat's smaller size enabled him to slip through the bars of the extra-large cell in which he had been placed when he was New, Improved, Giant Economy-Size Pie-Rat. Since the cell was designed to hold extra-large prisoners, the bars were spaced wide enough apart that, after sucking in a deep breath, Pie-Rat was able to squeeze through the bars to freedom. He gathered up the splintered pieces of Vetvix's power crystal, placed them into his pocket, and quietly slipped through the docking port and into the *Planetary Pizza*.

What kind of weirdo ship is this? he thought as he powered up the makeshift spacecraft. *Whatever it is, it was able to knock the power out of the* Lightspeed Lasagna *for a while, and that's good enough for me.*

Pie-Rat engaged the main engines in the *Planetary Pizza* and the ship shot away from the *Lightspeed Lasagna* like a bullet. He then pressed a "last number redial" button that Binky had installed on the ship's dashboard and the magic brew onboard once again sent out the command to shut off all the power on the *Lightspeed Lasagna*.

Pet Force awakened with a jolt at the sound of the *Planetary Pizza* blasting off, but by the time they could react, Pie-Rat had already sent the command to shut down the *Lightspeed Lasagna*'s engines.

"Can you get us any power?" Garzooka asked Compooky.

"Not for at least two hours, Garzooka," explained Compooky. "That's a pretty powerful spell we set up."

"Pie-Rat's getting away and he's got the power crystal," worried Abnermal.

"Well, it won't do him much good shattered into all those pieces," said Starlena.

"Starlena's right," said Garzooka. "Forget about Pie-Rat. The crystal is destroyed, and he won't get far in that ship anyway. When we get our power back, we'll head back to the *Menacing Moon of Mayhem* and see if we can find Vetvix. I only hope she's still there and still tiny."

13

On the *Menacing Moon of Mayhem*, Gorbull had finally cornered Vetvix. She was trapped. There was nowhere left to go.

"Get away from me!" squeaked the mini-Vetvix. "Good Gorbull, nice Gorbull!"

Gorbull bared his gleaming white teeth and opened his jaws wide — just as the magic reducing spell wore off. Vetvix shot up to her normal size and glared down at her pet. Gorbull slowly closed his jaws and backed away sheepishly.

"Where are you going, my pet?" cackled Vetvix, feeling evil magic surge through her body once again.

Gorbull turned and bolted down a hallway.

"You can run, but you can't hide!" shouted Vetvix. She released a spell that flooded the hallway with a sickly green magic energy. The spell struck Gorbull and he instantly transformed into a hamburger with four pitbull legs. The mobile burger continued to run, banging into walls as it went.

"Unless I miss my guess, those Pet Fools will come back here looking for me," said Vetvix to herself. "It's time to pack up this lab and hit the road — again!"

Sure enough, by the time the *Lightspeed Lasagna* had regained its power and Pet Force returned to the *Menacing Moon of Mayhem*, Vetvix had fled, leaving her former base an empty, deserted moon.

"Looks like we lost both Space Pie-Rat and Vetvix," said Garzooka.

"Yes, but we recovered the *Lightspeed Lasagna*," pointed out Starlena, "so it will be ready for us in case we're ever summoned back to this universe."

"And, of course, we rescued you from the evil spell that held you, Garzooka," added Compooky.

"I don't know," said Abnermal. "I kind of liked him evil. You know, the whole personality thing. I —"

Starlena glared at Abnermal.

"Kidding!" he said. "Just kidding!"

Pet Force then set their course for the planet Deli. After returning the stolen food and making a few apologies and repairs, they returned to Emperor Jon's palace on the planet Polyester.

"Once again I am grateful for your help," said the emperor as the five heroes prepared to return to their own universe. "I hope I don't have to see you again soon."

"The feeling is mutual, your highness," replied Garzooka. Then the five friends were once again sent through the dimensional portal by Sorcerer Binky.

Our universe, Jon's living room . . .

Garfield, Odie, Arlene, Nermal, and Pooky reemerged through the cover of *Pet Force #100*, and in a flash, they were back in the same positions they had been in when their latest adventure started.

Once again, practically no time had passed in this universe while they had been gone. Outside it was still raining.

Jon had dozed off on the couch in front of the television, right in the middle of *Here Come the Nerds, Part VI*. The return of Garfield and the others startled him, and he woke up yelling "Nerds rule!" an imitation of his favorite character from the movie.

Around here they do, that's for sure, thought Garfield as he resumed his boredom-busting game of counting the strawberries on the wallpaper, waiting for his nap to kick in.

Garfield was now certain that he and his friends would be summoned back to the parallel universe whenever danger struck — or whenever he was about to chow down on his fourth pan of lasagna of the day!

Epilogue

The parallel universe . . .

In a hidden laboratory somewhere deep in space, a diabolical experiment was taking place. Vet-vix turned up the power to the energization booth that now hummed with evil energy. "What was incomplete before will now be finished," she hissed and smiled a terrible smile.

Inside the booth stood the result of her latest sinister plan. He was called K-Niner. Once just an ordinary Doberman pinscher, K-Niner now stood upright like a human, nearly six feet tall. His already powerful body grew in strength from the energy that bombarded him in the booth. His ruthless, nasty personality — he was not a nice Doberman — was also enhanced.

K-Niner was receiving his final dose of brain-enhancing radiation. This treatment increased his intelligence to match his newly enhanced body. Finally, the treatment was finished. K-Niner emerged from the energization booth practically glowing with savage ferocity.

"It worked!" shouted Vetvix. "Now go, K-Niner, and set in motion my plan that will give me total control of Emperor Jon's universe!"

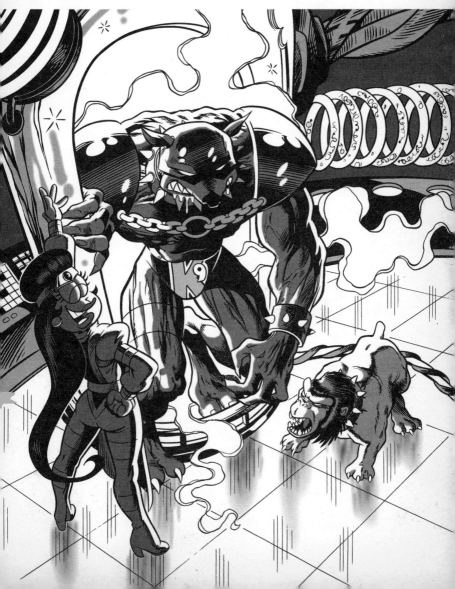